In loving memory of
my little JJ

Special thanks to:
My family, Cindy, and Lucas

This book is given with love to...

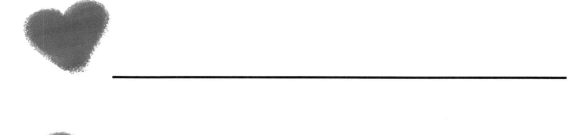

_____

_____

I'll be your Hero!

It's Okay to be Afraid

by Gayoung BB Yang

This is Jay.

Jay wanted nothing more than to be a superhero.

"Tap Tap Tap"

Every day, Jay said to himself,
"I am not afraid of anything!
I am not scared of anything!
I am the bravest boy this town has ever seen!"

On his fifth birthday, Jay received the best present he could have ever asked for...

...something that every great superhero needs.

A Sidekick!

But first, he needed a name.
"My noble sidekick, I hereby name you: Jay Junior.
JJ for short!"

Jay imagined all the exciting adventures and rescue missions that lay ahead of them.

And it didn't take long until it was time for Jay and JJ's first mission!

Let's GO!

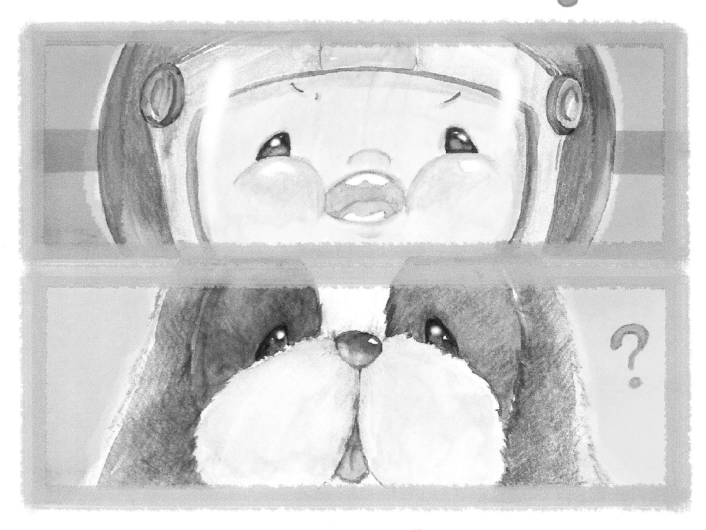

To the RESCUE!

Ee

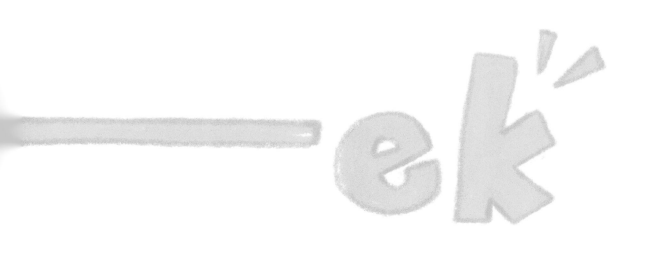

But, wait!
What happened?
Was JJ afraid of bigger dogs?

Can it be?
JJ was scared of little dogs, too?

...and of little steps?

...and of a little bath

...Even of his own little fart?

He felt so disappointed in JJ.

"My sidekick needs to be strong and brave,
but you are just a little scaredy pup.
I will never take you on any of my missions.
Not now, not ever!"

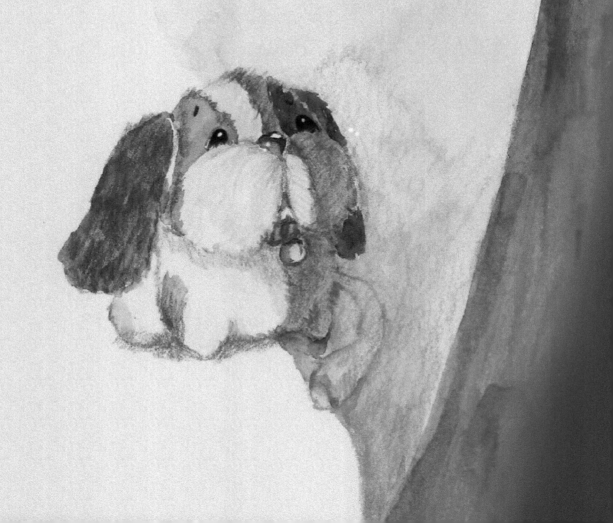

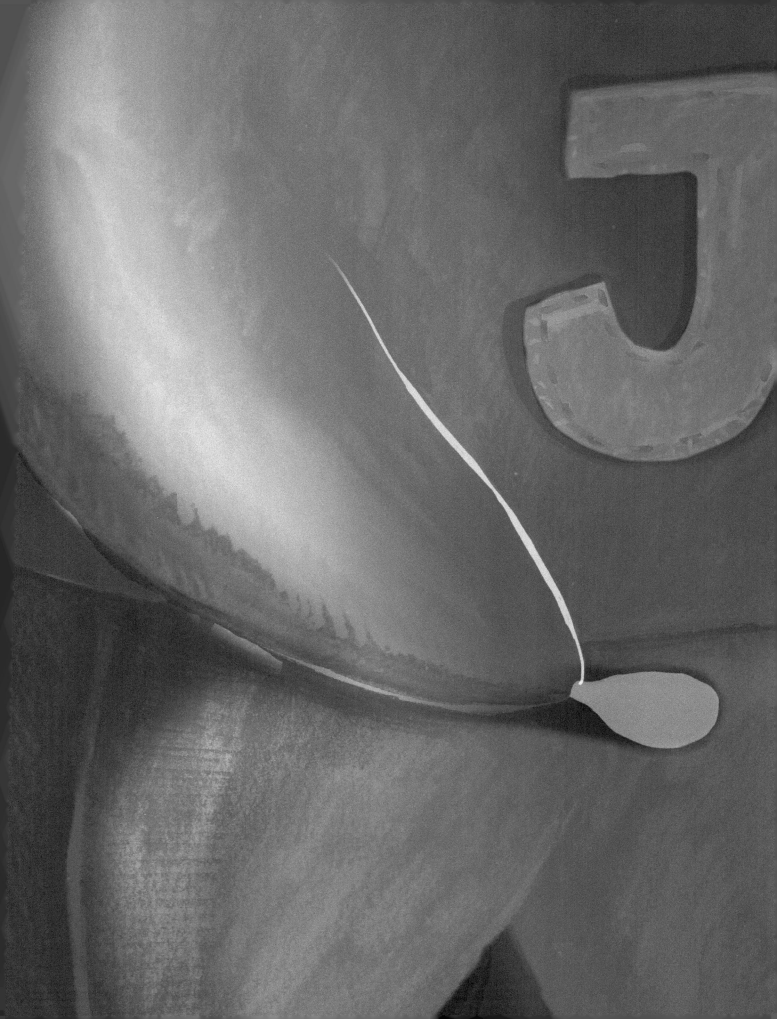

That night, Jay woke to crashing thunder
and flashes of lightning.

As he lay frightened in his bed, he said to himself,
"I am not afraid of anything!
I am not scared of anything!
I am the bravest boy this town has ever seen!"
But nothing would stop his trembling.

With an extra loud boom of thunder,
Jay leapt out of bed and ran to
his parents' room.

As he lay in his parents' bed,
he felt just like a little scaredy pup.
"Are you disappointed in me for
being afraid?" He asked.

His dad smiled and replied,
"We would never be disappointed in you.
You are the bravest boy we've ever seen.
You ran all the way across the hall on this
dark and stormy night!"

Jay's mum wrapped the blanket around him
and held him tight, until he stopped trembling.

Suddenly, Jay remembered JJ was all alone
on this dark and stormy night.

Jay then jumped out of his parents' bed and
rushed back across the hall
to his room where JJ was shaking with fear.

"I'm so sorry, JJ,
you must be so scared."

"I will never leave you again.
I will never call you a little scaredy pup.
And I promise I will always protect you!"

Jay wrapped the blanket around JJ and
held him tight, until JJ stopped trembling.

Hugging JJ made Jay feel warm and safe.
They weren't scared of the storm anymore
because they now had each other.

As they drifted off to sleep, Jay smiled and said,
"JJ, you are the best sidekick I could ever ask for."

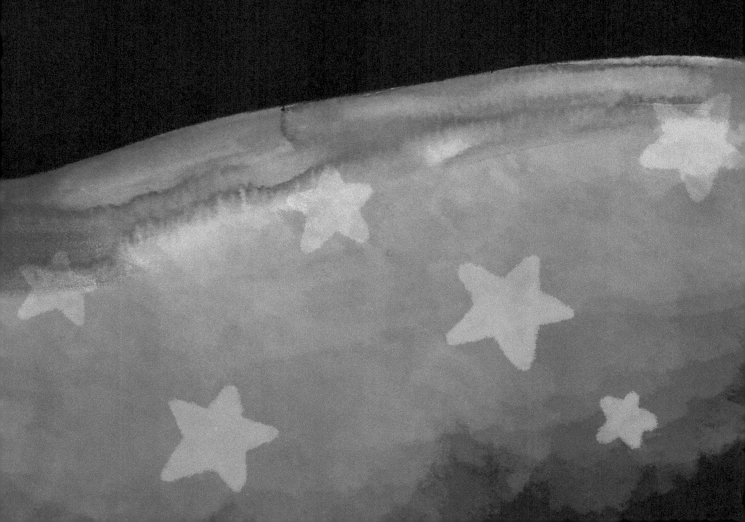

Jay learned that it's okay to be scared sometimes,
and how important it is to help your friends.

Now Jay and JJ go on lots of missions,
and know that they are both there for each other
if things get tough.

together forever!

Let's Draw!

Draw your greatest fear below,
and let SUPER JAY and JJ help you defeat it!

Let's Help Others!

People can be afraid of a lot of things.
What are some things that you can do or say
to help others feel better when they are scared?

About the Real-Life JJ

♥

JJune "JJ" was born in the winter 2003 on a small duck farm in South Korea. Gayoung's mom fell in love with him right away when she saw him and it was truly a miracle for Gayoung, because her mom wasn't a dog person at all.

JJune was a real scaredy pup, but it did not deter his family's love. Despite his fear, he ended up flying thousands of miles with Gayoung and spent the last half of his life in Vancouver, Canada learning the English dog language and trying new types of treats.

He enjoyed his last, beautiful summer in 2016 but continues to live on in Gayoung and her family's hearts as well as in this beloved story.

About the Author/Illustrator

Gayoung is a day dreamer, dog lover, cat envier, and an animator for the cartoon dog, Snoopy. Her love for children and animals drew her into creating heartwarming and funny books and illustrations. You can check her other work on her instagram @bbvineart.

About the Story Editor

Anita is a Vancouver Island born and raised artist, and now lives in Vancouver. Although the city is faster paced, she tries to embody slower lifestyle as much as possible.

She enjoys all formats of 2D art and is currently working in the Animation Industry as a compositor. When Anita is not working, she is hanging out with her dog Milo, her turtle Tristan, reading, or going on walks.

About the Line Editor

Chloe is a chatterbox who loves animals of all shapes and sizes; the fluffier the better! She hails from London, UK, where she produces television comedies.

Since moving to Canada, she can be found falling off her snowboard on the mountains, tripping over tree roots on Vancouver's various trails, and belly-flopping into freezing lakes. However, her favourite activity is cozying up on the sofa and laughing with friends. To the left you can see a young Chloe squeezing her long-suffering childhood dog, Abbey.

Claim your FREE Gift!

🐾 Visit: 🐾

PDICBooks.com/Gift

Thank you for purchasing

I'll Be Your Hero!

and welcome to the Puppy Dogs & Ice Cream family.
We're certain you're going to love the little gift
we've prepared for you at the website above.

CPSIA information can be obtained
at www.ICGtesting.com
Printed in the USA
BVHW090123101121
621202BV00018B/440